Ada Lace

and the
Suspicious Artist

Ada Lace

and the Suspicious Artist

• AN ADA LACE ADVENTURE •

EMILY CALANDRELLI

WITH TAMSON WESTON

ILLUSTRATED BY RENÉE KURILLA

Simon & Schuster Books for Young Readers

New York   London   Toronto   Sydney   New Delhi

For those who are brave enough to stick up for others
—E. C.

Fot the students at PS 63
—T. W.

For Ada's biggest fans: Grace Cotter, Sylvie Bargar,
and Grace Kelley
—R. K.

SIMON & SCHUSTER BOOKS FOR YOUNG READERS
An imprint of Simon & Schuster Children's Publishing Division
1230 Avenue of the Americas, New York, New York 10020
This book is a work of fiction. Any references to historical events, real people, or real places are used fictitiously. Other names, characters, places, and events are products of the author's imagination, and any resemblance to actual events or places or persons, living or dead, is entirely coincidental.
Text copyright © 2019 by Emily Calandrelli
Cover and interior illustrations copyright © 2019 by Renée Kurilla
All rights reserved, including the right of reproduction in whole or in part in any form.
SIMON & SCHUSTER BOOKS FOR YOUNG READERS
is a trademark of Simon & Schuster, Inc.
For information about special discounts for bulk purchases, please contact Simon & Schuster Special Sales at 1-866-506-1949 or business@simonandschuster.com.
The Simon & Schuster Speakers Bureau can bring authors to your live event. For more information or to book an event, contact the Simon & Schuster Speakers Bureau at 1-866-248-3049 or visit our website at www.simonspeakers.com.
Also available in a Simon & Schuster Books for Young Readers hardcover edition
Book design by Laurent Linn
The text for this book was set in Minister Std.
The illustrations for this book were rendered digitally.
Manufactured in the United States of America
0119 OFF
First Simon & Schuster Books for Young Readers paperback edition February 2019
2 4 6 8 10 9 7 5 3 1
Library of Congress Cataloging-in-Publication Data
Names: Calandrelli, Emily, author. | Weston, Tamson, author. | Kurilla, Renée, illustrator.
Title: Ada Lace and the suspicious artist / Emily Calandrelli ; with Tamson Weston ; illustrated by Renée Kurilla.
Description: First edition. | New York : Simon & Schuster Books for Young Readers, 2019. | Series: An Ada Lace adventure ; [5] | Summary: Eight-year-old Ada and new friend Tycho help Nina by coding a website displaying her online portfolio, then work together again to document a case of fraud.
Identifiers: LCCN 2018003729| ISBN 9781534416888 (hardcover) | ISBN 9781534416871 (pbk.) | ISBN 9781534416895 (eBook)
Subjects: | CYAC: Mystery and detective stories. | Web sites—Design—Fiction. | Computer programming—Fiction. | Fraud—Fiction. | Artists—Fiction. | Friendship—Fiction.
Classification: LCC PZ7.1.C28 Acm 2019 | DDC [Fic]—dc23 LC record available at https://lccn.loc.gov/2018003729

Ada Lace

and the
Suspicious Artist

Chapter One
A Man Named Miroir

Okay. A tick to the right," said Nina.

"I moved it to the right before, and you said to move it back," said Ada.

"Okay! Sorry! Wait a minute. Now I don't know if that background looks good with these pieces. Maybe we should start over."

"Nina!"

Ada was helping Nina build an online portfolio. It was the best way to introduce her creative energy to the universe, Nina had said. They had been at it all day, and patience was wearing thin. Ada had some of the coding skills, and Nina had a vision in her mind's eye, but making those two things meet in the middle was harder than they thought. All the numbers, letters, tags,

and brackets were starting to blur together. They had already spent an hour trying to add a feature that would allow art lovers to position an image of the piece they were thinking of buying within a picture of their space so they could see what it would look like in context. Ada had learned a few different coding languages from working on George, but Web design was a different ball game. She couldn't quite manage what Nina wanted. And since Ada couldn't perfect the art placement feature, Nina seemed unhappy with everything.

"I'm sorry," said Nina. "It's just that I want Nina Nina Land to look professional . . . impressive. I want Guy Miroir to know I'm for real."

That was the other problem. Ada was sick of this Miroir character. Her mom had been preparing for his show all week, and Ada had never seen her so stressed out. Between Ms. Lace and Nina, it seemed like Miroir was the only important person in the world. She looked forward to having her friend and her mom back.

"I'm not a professional," said Ada. "If I were, I would be charging you!"

In the middle of it all Elliott burst into Ada's room with socks on his hands and started rubbing the corner of her desk, her bookshelf, and the head of her bed.

"What are you doing, Elliott?" asked Ada.

"I'm helping clean!" said Elliott.

Mr. Lace popped his head in. "Elliott. You're supposed to be cleaning *your* room."

"Oh, I am," said Elliott. "I'm just making it fun!"

"It's not supposed to be fun. It's supposed to be done!" said Mr. Lace.

Elliott stomped out of Ada's room.

"I don't know how much more I can do," said Ada. "At least right now. This is beyond my skill level."

"Fine," said Nina. "I'm going to go home for a bit and see if I can come up with something a little simpler, I guess."

"You know, Mr. Peebles's nephew, Tycho, is

here," said Mr. Lace. "Isn't he a really good Web programmer?"

"Yes, he is!" said Ada. "Thanks, Dad."

Ms. Lace was at the gallery late again, so it was just Ada, Elliott, and Mr. Lace for dinner. Elliott insisted on cooking. It was his latest kick. Ada did not have high hopes. If she and Nina hadn't spent so much time together already, she would have gone to Nina's for dinner.

The table was set as only Elliott could set it— with a dinosaur in front of each plate. Ada sat in her usual seat.

"No, ADA! That's not your spot!" said Elliott. He was wearing a big poufy chef's hat and a gray apron that reached his toes.

"What do you mean? This is always my spot," said Ada.

"No, you're the *Stegosaurus*, obviously. *Dad's* the *Brachiosaurus*."

That did make sense somehow.

"But Dad's seat is always at the end," said Ada.

"Did *you* make dinner?" Elliott asked.

Ada sat behind the *Stegosaurus*. Elliott retreated into the kitchen. He came back out grasping a saucepan in two oversized, dirty yellow oven mitts. Just as he was about to reach Ada's seat, he tripped over one of the apron's table. Ada escaped almost unscathed, but for a few beans on her sweater. It was the perfect ending to a perfect day.

"OH NO!" yelled Elliott. "My masterpiece!"

Mr. Lace poked his head in and sighed.

"Mom just texted that she was on her way home," he said. "I'll tell her to bring a pizza from Donello's."

"I'm sorry, Dad," said Elliott.

"We'll try breakfast this weekend, Ell. And maybe we'll get you a better fitting apron."

An hour later they were seated around the pizza. Ms. Lace looked frazzled.

"I'm so glad to be here with you guys," said Ms. Lace.

"Bad day?" asked Ada.

"Well, it was challenging. Guy Miroir . . .

needs a lot of things. He didn't like any of the hotels in the city, so we had to put him up in Napa Valley. He's very . . . particular. You know how these artists can be."

"Tell me about it," said Ada, thinking of Nina.

Chapter Two
THE MASTER CODER

The next day Ada took her dad's advice and called Tycho to ask for help on Nina's website. After breakfast she crossed the courtyard to Mr. Peebles's stoop. She was about to ring the bell when Tycho shouted out the window from above.

"Hey, Ada, check this out."

After a few minutes the lock to the front door released. Ada stepped to the side to make way for the opening door. She was impressed. Last time she had visited Mr. Peebles's building, he could unlock the door with a button, but it couldn't open on its own. She entered the building and started to climb the stairs. But then, from behind the staircase, she heard a loud, metallic clank and a squeaking sound. The tips of Tycho's sneakers

were just visible descending behind the staircase.
There was an elevator back there now! It didn't
look like a normal elevator though. There was an
old-school, handmade feel to it. After another

clank, Alan jumped from Tycho's lap and ran toward Ada. Tycho wheeled behind. Ada clapped.

"That's amazing!"

"I know! We finished it right after I got here."

Ada had met Tycho a few months before when he had come to stay for a long weekend with Mr. Peebles. It had been tough. Mr. Peebles had to have help from their neighbor Jacob or Mr. Lace to get Tycho and his wheelchair up and down the stairs. But now they had a manual elevator based on an old Otis design. That and the automatic door meant that Tycho could come and go as he pleased.

"Can I ride on it?" asked Ada.

"Of course!"

Ada ran over to the elevator. There was a rope that was kept taut to keep the elevator from moving. In order to go up, Tycho tugged on the rope to release the brake. Then Ada pulled on the other rope to make it go up. They moved about a foot off the ground and stopped.

"That's hard!" she said, shaking out her arms.

"I got you," said Tycho.

He handily pulled them to the top of the stairs. Ada set the rope for the brake.

"I can't believe you could do that," she said. "My arms feel like spaghetti."

"Well, mine get a lot of work," said Tycho. "Come on, I want to show you something."

Alan jumped into the chair beside Tycho and gnawed away contentedly on his chewy. Ada opened the door to Mr. Peebles's apartment and they went inside.

"Alan looks pretty cozy there," said Ada.

"Yeah," said Tycho. "I've been giving him free rides since I got here!"

Alan looked up at Tycho and licked his fingers. Then he nestled in and started chewing again. Tycho rolled into Mr. Peebles's workshop and Ada followed. Spread across the floor was a lot of hardware—big wheels with knobby tires, metal piping, PVC, nuts, bolts, and various kinds of jigs.

"Ta-da!" said Tycho, as if the magic were clear.

"Uhh . . . cool? What am I looking at?"

"Oh, uh"—he looked around—"the plans are over there." He pointed to a piece of paper anchored under a couple of bolts. It showed a really rugged looking rig, with big knobby tires and handlebars in the front.

"It's a handcycle! Kinda like a bicycle with three big wheels, but instead of pedaling with my feet, I turn these cranks with my hands. The best part is that it can roll over all kinds of terrain. I want to go mountain biking." Tycho lowered his voice. "The next step will be convincing my mom."

"Wow, that's amazing! When will it be ready?"

Just then Mr. Peebles walked in, wiping his hands with a rag.

"Hopefully, by the end of the week?" said Mr. Peebles. "It'll be tight, but we're trying."

"Well, we should plan a hiking trip to celebrate," said Ada.

"Good idea!" said Tycho.

"I guess that's my cue to go finish cutting those jigs," said Mr. Peebles. "Good to see you, Ada."

He left the room, and Ada could hear the sound of metal grinding.

"So, you need a little help with that online portfolio?" said Tycho.

"Do I ever," said Ada.

Ada explained that Nina wanted to let visitors to the site see what her artwork would look like on their wall by uploading a picture of their room and then dragging and dropping her artwork into place.

"Hmmm . . . that's tricky. Sounds like a great feature for a portfolio though. I think I can figure it out. I'll check a few coding forums and see if anyone else has tried to build something like this before. Give me a little time with it," said Tycho.

"Great! I really appreciate it. Can you show me how you did it afterward?" asked Ada.

"Absolutely! It's nice to find a friend who appreciates the art of coding," said Tycho.

Ada had to agree. They made plans to meet the next day.

Chapter Three

FUNDAMENTAL MOOD

Does my breath smell funny?" asked Nina.

"For the tenth time: No!" said Ada. "You smell good, you look good—very artsy. Would you relax! He's just a person."

"A person who is changing the face of twenty-first century art as we know it! A person who seems to have invented his own palette and sense of shape! He's a person, yes, Ada. But not just *anyone!*"

"All right, all right," said Ada. "But try to calm down anyway."

They were going to a reception to welcome Guy Miroir. This was really just a meet and greet before his big show—none of his art would be on display yet—but it was a chance for his biggest fans, and potential buyers of his artwork, to meet the man behind the canvas. Nina couldn't contain herself. She'd been trying to make a scarf for Miroir for the past three weeks and had driven Ada crazy with all the different versions of it. First, she based it on a piece of Miroir's called *Fundamental Mood*. It was various shades of red, but mostly looked brown to Ada, because of her color blindness. Of course, she knew she couldn't tell Nina that. Still, even though Ada had assured her friend numerous times that the scarf was beautiful, Nina didn't believe her. She rejected it and started over. The next one was based on a different piece from the same series, called *Casual Fright*. The scarf was all bright green with flecks of white, Ada thought. Of course, if they were light pink, she wouldn't have known it. That one was rejected too. Ada suspected there might have been more attempts, but Nina finally settled on a blue scarf. This one had different shades of blue, and if you looked at it up close, there were little points of yellow, like stars. It wasn't based on any of Miroir's work. It was Nina's own design.

"That's lovely," said Ada when she saw it.

"Yeah, I think I finally got it right. I just hope Guy likes it," said Nina. "He's known for his scarves."

Ada had already heard about the scarves from Nina. In fact, she'd heard about it every time she presented a new one.

"And plus, the scarf is just the intro! Once he sees I'm an artist, Guy will probably ask to see my portfolio." It was obvious that Nina was getting a bit ahead of herself.

"You might want to call him Mr. Miroir," said Ada's mom. "I think he prefers it."

"Oh yes," said Nina. "I'm sure first names will come soon enough. We are destined to be friends. I can feel our creative energies complementing each other already!"

"It's important to be able to separate the art from the artist, Nina," said Ms. Lace.

But Nina wasn't paying attention. She was folding the scarf and refolding it. First she put it in a box and tied a ribbon around it, and then she wondered if it would be better to give it to Mr. Miroir tied up like a swan. Then she thought maybe she should just be casual. Every time she tried a new form of presentation, she asked for Ada's opinion. Every single time Ada approved. But it didn't matter. Nina wasn't really looking for an answer.

As they approached the gallery, Ms. Lace told the girls and Mr. Lace to go in the front without her. She had to meet Guy Miroir in the back room.

"Remember, this event is invite-only, and please, make sure your phones are put away. Mr. Miroir has very strict requirements for any public appearances."

"Oh, why don't I go with you, Ms. Lace?" said Nina. "You know, in case Guy . . . uh . . . Mr. Miroir needs some extra company."

"I don't think so, Nina," said Ms. Lace. "Mr. Miroir was very clear about just meeting me. You'll be able to give him your gift. Just give us some time."

"Oh, but we'll have so much to talk about!" said Nina.

"Nina," said Ms. Lace. "Not now."

Ada noticed her mother's jaw clench just a little bit. She knew that Ms. Lace loved Nina, so she guessed there must be something else wrong. Nina noticed too.

"Is your mom okay?" asked Nina.

"She's been a little stressed out," said Ada. "Miroir is probably the biggest artist she's brought to her gallery. She even said the mayor might come to see him tonight. Tensions are high."

"Well, Mr. Miroir has a lot of fans," said Nina.

"Yes," said Mr. Lace. "And a lot of demands."

Chapter Four
THE ARTIST REVEALED

Nina was just as hyper inside the gallery. She talked Ada's ear off about her favorite pieces in the Miroir collection.

"Oh, I hope we get to see *Fundamental Mood*. He painted it when he was living in the Southwest. You can tell by the colors. Oh! Oh! And *The Clearest Night*. He created that one in his twenties when he was on a boat in the middle of the ocean!"

Ada actually didn't mind. She was impressed that her friend knew so much about this artist's work and about art in general. Plus, she felt like she was studying up for Miroir's grand opening next week. Nina was just explaining the influence of the artist Rothko on a particular piece when they heard a shattering noise followed by a loud, annoyed voice.

"CAN'T YOU READ?? The sign says clearly NO CAMERAS. And you were bold enough to use a FLASH?? My eyes are my life. Are you trying to kill me??"

Both girls turned to look. Ada saw her mom bending down to pick up someone's phone. She handed it back to the upset photographer with a comforting pat to the shoulder. The man next to her continued to bellow.

"You don't deserve to be here if you can't follow directions. Everybody is just running around breaking rules and blinding innocent artists now, I suppose!"

The artist was dressed in overalls with a bright pink shirt underneath. He had on short black work boots and one of the signature scarves Ada

had heard so much about was tied around his neck in a loose knot.

Just as he was wrapping up his rant, the mayor arrived, surrounded by a crowd of people in suits. Mr. Miroir elbowed his way to her side. It seemed he had forgotten all about the clumsy photographer. He bowed his head and took the mayor's hand, smiling and oozing charm, as if he hadn't just been shrieking and making a scene. Ada knew from her mom that the mayor was looking for a new piece to hang in her office. Based on how Mr. Miroir was schmoozing her up, Ada bet that he wanted *his* art selected for that prime real estate.

"Geez," said Ada. "Can you believe that guy?"

"I know, right?" said Nina. "How can he not know that cameras aren't allowed at Miroir shows! It's his thing. No cameras. He wants his artwork to create 'internal expression.'"

"Are you kidding?" said Ada. "He was so mean!"

"Well, you heard him, Ada," said Nina. "His eyes are his life!"

"Seems a little dramatic," said Ada.

"You wouldn't understand," said Nina.

"I guess not," said Ada.

She had met a lot of artists her mom worked with. She had never known one of them to raise their voice or even make an angry face. She had also never seen her mom so stressed out around any of them. She didn't act the same as she did with Ada and Elliott, but she seemed to enjoy their company.

"You know there's a lot of pressure that comes with . . ."

Before Nina finished her sentence, Ada's mom and Miroir had joined them.

"Mr. Miroir, I'd like you to meet my husband, Byron, my daughter, Ada, and her friend . . ."

"Yes, yes. Very nice. Very cute, Isabella. Charmed! Now could I possibly get some room-temperature water before I collapse from dehydration?"

"Of course. It's just that Nina here is a big fan. She has something for you," said Ms. Lace in a very patient tone.

"Oh, I suppose it's another scarf, right? Very sweet, dear, but I have more than I can wear! Now, about that water."

"But, Mr. Miroir, it's not just a scarf! It's an original scarf! I have an entire portfolio online called Nina Nina Land! It has . . ." Before she could finish, Mr. Miroir already had his back to her, walking toward another guest.

Nina looked crushed. As they walked away,

Ms. Lace looked back at them sadly and mouthed, "Sorry."

"He didn't even look at it! I've spent so much time looking at his paintings. I infused so much of my artistic soul into this fabric! He didn't even peek," said Nina.

"Nina," said Ada. She touched her friend's shoulder. Nina just shrugged it off and headed toward the bathroom.

"Poor Nina," said Mr. Lace.

Ada looked down at the floor. The scarf Nina made was sitting there in a heap. She picked it up, folded it just as Nina had done before, and placed it neatly in her backpack.

Chapter Five

PEP TALK

The trip home from the gallery that night was quiet. Ada wanted to reassure Nina, but it was no use.

The next morning Ada tried to call Nina, but she was still asleep. Nina was usually up way before Ada. In fact, Ada had to make a rule that she not call on weekends earlier than eight. It was almost nine already.

Elliott was making French toast for breakfast. George alerted Ada to the emergency.

"Fire! Fire! Leave the house immediately!" said the robot, rolling back and forth down the hallway. Luckily, Ada had disconnected him from the sprinkler system after he set it off for the third time last month.

"The fire is out, George!" called Ada. George rolled back into his corner and shut down.

"Ada!" yelled Elliott. "Breakfast!"

"Yeah! I can smell it! So can George!"

She made her way down to the kitchen and sat behind the *Stegosaurus*. Mom was behind the *Triceratops*, reading over some paperwork.

"Good morning, Ada-Beta," she said.

"Morning."

Elliott placed a plate in front of Ada. The French toast looked perfect. It was a golden color, cut into perfect triangles, and garnished with a cut strawberry.

"Wow, Elliott," said Ada. "This looks delicious."

"It probably is!" said Elliott. "I only burned one side!"

Ada lifted up the corner of her toast. It was

black underneath. She looked at her mom, who smiled and shrugged. Ada did her best to cut off the burned bits and eat the rest.

After breakfast, Ada called Nina's house again. It was ten o'clock and Nina still wasn't awake. An hour later Ada called again. Ms. Scarborough said Nina wasn't ready to leave her room. Finally, Ada just went over.

"I'm so glad you came," said Nina's mom. "Nina could use a pep talk."

"I'll do my best, Ms. Scarborough," said Ada, "but I haven't helped so far. And I don't have nearly the pep Nina usually has."

"If you can just get her out of her room, that would be some progress," said Ms. Scarborough.

Ada walked into her friend's room. All of the artwork had been changed since the last time she'd been in there. There were new paintings spread all over the desk, and Nina had made new mobiles, which were hanging from the ceiling. A few of the rejected scarves Nina made were still tied to the headboard of her bed. Ada may not have been good with color, but she could see that they were in rainbow order. In the corner a half-finished quilt hung over the chair. Nina was on her bed, holding a tablet. She hadn't even changed out of her pajamas yet.

"Neens, you're still in bed? Don't you want to take a big, bold step into the beautiful world?" This

was something Nina said all the time. Ada never thought she would ever hear herself saying it.

"Pffft. Yeah, right. Like I would know what beauty is," said Nina.

"What are you talking about?" Ada sat on the bed next to her friend. Nina had a game of solitaire open on her tablet. Ada waved her hand in front of Nina's face as if to break a spell. "Look at this room! Look at all the things you've made! Who knows what's beautiful better than you do?!"

"A very famous artist by the name of Guy Miroir. That's who."

"The only thing that Guy seems to know better than you do is how to make good people feel lousy. He's been torturing my mom for three weeks straight, and now he's hurt you, too. When I look at his art now, all I see is mean."

"Really?"

"Absolutely."

Nina closed the solitaire game and opened up a large book Ms. Lace had given to her that included pieces of Miroir's.

"Huh. That's funny. They still look beautiful to me," said Nina. "But maybe your mom's right. Maybe I just need to focus on the art and forget about the artist."

"Exactly," said Ada. "But if you want to skip the show tomorrow and hang out with me at home and watch movies, I'm game." She crossed her fingers behind her back. She really didn't want to see that man again.

"Nah. I still want to see his new stuff," said Nina. "Will you still go with me?"

"Of course," Ada said. "Also, I talked to Tycho earlier, and he's found the code he needed to make your portfolio work. We should go see!

Miroir might not be interested, but you know how exclusive his shows are—there may just be another artistic genius dying to see it!"

"Yeah, you might be right!"

Chapter Six

TYCHO'S MAGIC

Nina and Ada went to Mr. Peebles's place to talk to Tycho. Mr. Peebles's lab was still crammed with hardware from the wheelchair project. There had been a path about wheelchair width cleared from the doorway to the desk and around the edge of the room, but the rest of the floor was covered in metal parts.

Tycho opened up the latest version of Nina's portfolio and showed Ada some of the code he used to implement the new features.

"I've made comments throughout the code explaining what each command does," Tycho explained. "Most of this I found online from someone who had already created something similar. I just tweaked it a bit."

It suddenly seemed so much simpler to Ada with his explanations. She wished she'd known that sometimes you can just find the code you need from a basic Google search. You don't always have to reinvent the wheel (or the website!). That's what was great about the coding community—they were usually willing to share their work.

"Your old site is still up now. This is a saved version of the new one. But if you're okay with what I've done, we can make this one live today," Tycho told Nina.

"Great!" said Nina.

He opened up the front page of Nina's portfolio, which still looked essentially the same. He scrolled through Nina's artwork and clicked on a painting. On the top of the page, Ada noticed there was an addition to the toolbar. It said *Show This Piece*.

"So you just click here," said Tycho, "and you have the option to upload a photo of your space."

He uploaded a photo of Mr. Peebles's lab.

"Then you enter the dimensions of the wall here." He entered ten feet by twelve feet into the appropriate box. "Voilà!" The painting appeared in the picture of the lab. It showed what it would look like over the workbench where they were sitting. But it completely blocked the window in the photo.

"Wow. That painting looks great over the workbench," said Ada.

Tycho laughed. "Yeah, we don't really need that window anyway! Once it's in there, though, you can move it wherever. Just drag it around until it's where you want it." He dragged it so it was next to the window.

"It's even better than I imagined!" said Nina. "Thanks so much, Tycho."

"Well, you know, Ada did a great job on this site. She made it really easy for me."

"Thank you, Ada," said Nina. Ada smiled gratefully at Tycho.

"It looks like you already have a bit of traffic for the site you have up already," said Tycho. "And with these new headings I've included, the new site will have much better SEO, so you should see more traffic right away."

Ada and Nina read some of the new title tags on her page: *San Francisco Artwork, San Francisco Local Young Artist, Affordable Artwork in the City.*

"What's SEO?" asked Nina.

"Search engine optimization," said Ada. "It just means that people who search for things similar to those headings will have an easier time finding your page through Google."

"Cool!"

They spent some time refining things. By the end of an hour the site was ready to go, and Nina seemed back to her happy self.

"Who needs Guy Miroir?" she said.

"So, you think we should skip the opening?" said Ada.

"Not a chance," said Nina. "Your mom was right. I need to separate the artist from the artwork. Miroir may have been having a bad day, but I still love his work."

Ada sighed.

Chapter Seven

MIROIR IMAGE

Guy Miroir seemed less cranky at the show. Perhaps because now he was surrounded by his best pieces of work. He looked . . . pleased with himself. He wore a black button-down shirt with pink polka dots and fitted jeans with the same black boots as before. Ada saw Nina look at him and swallow. Despite all her brave talk, she was still hurt that her hero didn't recognize her as a kindred spirit. Nina turned away and went into the next room. Ada decided to let her go.

The gallery was packed. Everyone was well dressed and very important looking. Most of the people were either talking to Guy or waiting to talk to him. A few were milling around the room looking at the art. Her mother had said that most of the pieces were old and borrowed from other collectors. Only a few were new.

Ada eventually found her way to Nina, who was standing in front of a very large piece called *Gleam amidst the Gloom*. It looked a little familiar. Nina had her head tilted, with a confused look on her face.

"Huh," said Ada. "This looks familiar?"

"Yeah," said Nina. "I'm not surprised." Ada's dad walked up just then.

"Mr. Lace," Nina asked, "can I borrow your phone? I want to show Ada something."

"Yes, just don't use the camera," Mr. Lace said in a hushed voice as he glanced over his shoulder. "I don't want to face the wrath of Mr. Miroir."

Mr. Lace entered his password and handed the phone to Nina. Nina typed in the URL for her online portfolio and scrolled through until

she found what she needed. Then she handed
the phone to Ada.

"Whoa," said Ada. There in the portfolio was
an almost exact replica of the piece in front of
them.

"Okay," Ada said slowly, "I know
I don't have your eye, but this looks exactly the

same to me. How is that possible, Nina?"

"Look, my piece is a different proportion than Miroir's, and some of the shapes here and here are a little different . . . I think." Nina pointed to different parts of the painting on the wall, but still had that scrunched up look on her face.

Mr. Lace studied the painting. "Nina, is it possible that you saw an earlier version of this painting and perhaps were inspired by it? Sometimes art can seep into our subconscious," he said.

"I never saw this piece before tonight," said Nina.

"Yeah, Nina did this piece a while ago, Dad," said Ada. "It's been in her portfolio since I started working on it."

"Hmmm . . . well, many pieces may seem similar because the artists have shared interests and influences. Let's not jump to conclusions just yet, ladies. We'll discuss this later," said Mr. Lace. He took his phone back, still staring at the image, and walked to the next room.

Nina was still frozen, staring at the all-too-familiar painting.

"He stole this from me!" said Nina.

"Maybe," said Ada. She put her hand on her friend's shoulder and lowered her voice. "But my dad has a point. It could be a hard thing to prove. It seems to me they're a tad too similar for it to be a coincidence, but we should look into this more."

Chapter Eight
The Case against Miroir

Ada and Nina knew what they were up against. Both of Ada's parents didn't seem to believe that Miroir would have stolen from Nina—he was too big of a name to risk something like that. They were convinced that Nina had seen an earlier version of Miroir's work, even though she didn't remember it. Nina and Ada were going to have to build a solid case to convince her parents that Nina had come up with the artwork first. Of course, the last case they tried to solve had gone slightly off the rails. But now Ada had a secret weapon: Tycho. Websites had a way of tracking who visited them and where those visitors came from. Nina's website would be no different, and Tycho would know how to retrieve that digital trail. So Ada and Nina went to see him.

Tycho opened a page with analytics on Nina's website.

"Okay, this shows the IP addresses of your website's visitors. An IP address is the way the Internet identifies computers. It's a pretty good way to learn more about the people visiting your website," he said.

"Can you tell who these visitors are?" Ada asked.

"Not *who* necessarily, but *where*. I just take those IP addresses and input them into this special website that will give you the latitude and longitude for the general location where they're using their computer.

"Just copy and paste those coordinates into Google Maps and—voilà! It'll show what city they're using their computer in. It's not always perfect, but it's not going to be too far off," said Tycho. "There's a lot of action in the city of San Francisco in general, which we would expect. Also, a lot from Palm Beach."

"That's where my Nana Kay lives!" said Nina.

"Well, it looks like she's telling all her friends about your portfolio. Now, this one's interesting. A ton of traffic from Napa Valley. Does that make sense to you?"

"Hmm. Not really. . . . I don't know anyone up there," said Nina.

"Interesting. And look here," he said, pointing to a series of numbers representing one IP address. That Napa Valley IP address appeared many, many times—more than any other string of numbers.

"Whoa," Ada said, pointing to the screen.

"This IP address accessed your website almost a hundred times."

"And you're sure you don't know anyone in Napa Valley, Nina?" Tycho asked.

Ada gasped. "*I* do." She turned to Nina. "Mr. Miroir didn't think the hotels in San Francisco were good enough for him. So, guess where my mom put him up?"

"Napa Valley!" Nina said.

"Bingo."

Ada's mom was still frazzled. Ada had been trying all morning to get her attention, but Ms. Lace was busy talking to potential clients and setting up meetings for Guy Miroir. Nothing usually seemed to rattle her, but after spending so much time with the demanding artist, the wear was starting to show. She picked up a pen and dropped it, put down a piece of paper and then lost it, dialed part of a phone number and then put the phone down. Maybe what Ada and Nina had to tell her would be a relief. Maybe Ms. Lace could just tell everyone about Guy Miroir once and for all—today—and then she wouldn't have to run around doing a bunch of chores for him.

Ada and Nina stood at the door to Ms. Lace's home office and watched as she shuffled a bunch of papers and circled, scratched out, and under-

lined various things with her pen. Finally, she looked up.

"Okay, girls. I know you've been following me. Out with it. Is this about the piece you think Guy stole from you, Nina?"

"Oh! He's *Guy* now," said Ada. "I thought it was Mr. Miroir."

"Just tell me what's up, please."

"It is about that piece," said Nina.

"Listen, I know it seems weird," said Ms. Lace. "But it happens all the time creatively. You are into the same things. You admire his work. . . ."

"But he made his piece *after* mine, Ms. Lace," said Nina.

"You don't know that for sure," said Ms. Lace.

"But we know he was looking at Nina's piece!" said Ada. "The IP address points to Napa Valley."

"Okay. I don't know about that, but even if he did, that doesn't mean he stole it. That's an incredibly serious accusation, I'm sure you're aware. I'm sorry, girls. I don't have any more time for this. I have to get back to the gallery." Ms. Lace grabbed her bag and left.

"That didn't go like I thought it would," said Ada.

"I know! She doesn't even like *Mr.* Miroir," said Nina. "Why is she covering for him?"

"I don't think she's covering for him. I just think she's not seeing it clearly. The show seems like a big success, and he's very respected. We're just going to have to find something more convincing."

Chapter Nine
NEW WHEELS

Ada needed a break from all the art drama. And a break from art in general. It was fine in small doses, but for the past week and a half it seemed like all she thought about was paintings. She wanted to talk to someone about technology and gadgets for a while. Someone who loved those things as much as she did. She decided to pay a visit to Tycho and Mr. Peebles to see how the handcycle was coming together. Tycho offered to hoist Ada up in the elevator, and she took him up on it. Normally, she always took the stairs when she could, to save electricity. But this elevator was Tycho powered, and Tycho power was good, green energy.

When she walked into Mr. Peebles's workroom, there was still a lot of stuff lying around,

but the chair did look like it was nearly put together.

"Does it work yet?" asked Ada. "Can we go hiking now?"

"Yes and no. It rolls, but the shocks aren't right yet, so it would be a pretty rough ride going off-road. Also, see that small wheel in the front?"

"Yeah?"

"That's what we use to steer, and for some reason it sticks sometimes. I would probably end up rolling around in a circle while you guys ran off down the trail. Soon, though, soon. Do you want to see how it works?"

"Yes!"

Ada went down on the elevator with the off-road wheelchair, and Tycho took a second trip with his regular wheelchair. When they got to the courtyard, Ada watched as Tycho transferred himself from the chair to the handcycle. Then, before she knew it, he was halfway down Juniper Garden with Alan yapping along behind him. He wheeled around in a circle at the opposite end and zoomed back toward her. It seemed like he was back within a minute.

"Wow," said Ada. "That was so fast!"

"Wanna try?" asked Tycho.

"I can?" asked Ada.

"Sure!"

Tycho shifted back to his wheelchair, and Ada climbed into the handcycle.

"Now, just use both hands and turn that crank forward," said Tycho.

Ada moved across Juniper Garden. It was a smoother ride than she was expecting. Like a bicycle, but more stable. This handcycle had three wheels instead of two, so that made sense.

"Wow, this thing really gets moving!" Ada yelled over her shoulder.

"You may want to slow do—" Before Tycho could finish, Ada's panic set in.

"The brake! Tycho! Where's the brake?!" That was one important detail he'd forgotten to tell her before she hopped on. Tycho had yelled something to Ada, but she couldn't hear him. A busy street was within her line of sight.

Think, Ada. Think. How would I brake on a basic bicycle? Ada thought to herself. She could hear the busy street looming closer.

"Backward!" Ada said out loud.

She turned the crank in the opposite direction, and the bike slowed down. Ada stopped just in time to see a semitruck zip in front of her. She turned to see Tycho wheeling down the hill, trying to catch up to her.

"You okay?! I forgot to tell you about the brakes. I'm so sorry," Tycho said breathlessly.

"Ya! What a ride!" Ada said, laughing.

Ada got out of the handcycle, and Tycho shifted back in to bring it up the hill. Then Nina, waving her tablet, came down the road.

"You guys! I found it!" said Nina. "We can prove Guy was a thief!"

Chapter Ten
The Evidence Mounts

Look here. These are all of Guy Miroir's mentions on Twitter over the past year. He has a ton of fans, and if you click on their profiles you can see that many of them are artists themselves. Like this man. He tweeted at Guy and the gallery in DC holding his show."

> Rob SanGogh @RobTheArtistSanGogh:
>
> Can't wait to meet my favorite artist in
>
> person! You're such an inspiration
>
> @miroirdelame. @DCartists

"Well, after I saw that Rob was an artist, I found his online portfolio, and in it was *this* piece," said Nina showing Ada and Tycho the art. "Honestly, it was the best piece he had in there, but still!" The piece was a deep midnight blue color with a bright pink circle floating at its center. It was abstract, but it felt like it had some depth to it.

"This tweet was posted about a month out from a show Guy Miroir had in DC." Nina pointed to the time stamp on the tweet and then switched tabs and pointed to the date of the DC show.

"Okay," said Ada.

"And then! What do you know?! Guy had *this* brand-new piece in the show."

Nina clicked over to Miroir's piece. It was similar, but, again, not exactly the same. The shape in the center was more of a full orb—almost planetlike, Ada thought. The hue looked a little different, although it was hard for Ada to judge, and the surrounding color was grayer. But the resemblance was strong—almost exact.

"Just like what happened to you," said Ada.

"Let's do a little more digging," said Tycho. "If we find a few more examples like that, we'll have a pattern. . . ."

"We'll have that fraud right where we want him!" Nina said.

The next day Nina met Ada at her house. Among Nina, Tycho, and Ada, they had five more pieces of art to consider. The craziest part was that they reached out to each of the artists, and all were aware of what had happened. Nina asked them why they hadn't come forward. Two of them said they tried, but no one would listen to them. The others said they were too afraid to say anything. The stolen pieces weren't exact replicas, plus, Guy Miroir was too big of an artist with too much influence in the art world. One word from Miroir and no one would be interested in featuring their work again.

"We've got to tell your mom," said Nina. "Where is she?"

"She's at the gallery," said Ada. "She and Miroir are preparing to meet the mayor."

"Perfect! I have an idea."

Chapter Eleven

MIROIR'S DEFENSE

Ada convinced her dad to bring them into town with him while he and Elliott ran errands. He said they could have a hot chocolate in the café next to the gallery. That way Ada's mom would be close by. Nina wanted to head over as soon as Ada's dad left, but Ada convinced her to wait so they could talk things out before they talked to

Ms. Lace and Miroir. She understood why Nina was angry, but she also knew if they went in hot, they were bound to get themselves in trouble.

"Okay," said Ada. "Once more. If we walk in there and Guy Miroir is with my mom . . ."

"Then I say, 'Hello, Mr. Miroir. I'm glad you're here. I wanted to ask you about your piece *Gleam amidst the Gloom.*'"

"Good. And if he denies that he took the idea from you?"

"Then we . . . bring in reinforcements."

"Right. I bet he'll be nervous right away though. Don't worry," said Ada. "He'll start getting defensive and give himself away. Then we've got him. Just stay cool, okay?"

"Okay."

By the time they got to the gallery, the clients had gone, and there was no one but Miroir and

Ms. Lace. Ada was relieved. She and Nina made their way to the back, where Ms. Lace's office was. Ms. Lace was seated at her desk, looking very tired. Guy was pacing and talking. He held his glasses in one hand and pinched the bridge of his nose with the other. His eyes were closed.

"Now, as you know, the mayor has decided to feature my piece *Gleam amidst the Gloom* in her office. You'll need to hurry up and pack that up for her—she'll be here any moment to pick it up. You know how many influential people will see my work because of this? You seem like a clumsy person, so don't screw it up for me."

That was the last straw for Nina. Before Ada knew what was happening, Nina burst into the room.

"You stole my work! That painting was my creation!" she yelled. So much for staying cool. Ada

continued to hide behind the door, while Nina stood before Miroir with her arms crossed. Ms. Lace's face dropped into her hands.

Guy's eyes popped open. He glared at Nina. Ada assumed he would start yelling, but instead Miroir laughed.

"Hahahaha. *Steal*. The very idea. Who is this charming little girl, Isabella?"

"Mr. Miroir, this is Nina Scarborough, my daughter's friend. You met her at the welcome reception."

"You may know me better as the person you stole that painting from! You know, the one that's going to the mayor?" Nina said defiantly.

"Well, my dear, if I'm a thief, then we both are. In fact, we're all thieves, we artists. At least the good ones. That's what Picasso would say, anyway, that old hack."

"How dare you!"

"Oh, I know, everyone loves Picasso. . . ."

"No! How dare you steal from me?!"

"Oh, you dear, sweet girl. You entertain me. Why is it you think I stole from you?"

Ada stepped into the office, armed with a portfolio of high resolution printouts.

"We can prove that you were looking at Nina's

work. We have analytics that show you looked at her painting more than a hundred times before you made your own *copy*. We can also prove that you have done the same thing with at least five other artists.

"These pieces," said Ada, laying out the evidence, "were created by admirers of Miroir.

"And *these* are pieces that Miroir made after seeing them." She presented the printouts of the Miroir copies. "Again, we have the digital trail that shows they were created after the originals."

"You'll notice that they are almost exact copies," Nina said, "but *Mr.* Miroir changed one little thing. I guess so he could get away with being a fraud."

Ms. Lace's face went white. Her jaw dropped. She looked sideways at Miroir, but the artist didn't seem fazed. He looked at each piece and smiled.

"Ah yes, I know these wonderful artists," said Miroir. "As you say, each is an admirer of my work, and their admiration has been rewarded in turn."

"WHAT?!" Nina was flabbergasted.

"You're right. Each piece is a mirror image, Nina. Good eye. I'm *reflecting* their work to a higher level. Without me, their creative vision

would have gone unnoticed. Don't you see? Well, anyway, it's not my job to explain the purpose of art to you."

"And what about me, Mr. Miroir?" They turned to see the mayor standing in the doorway. Her arms were crossed. "Would you like to explain the purpose of art *to me*?"

Chapter Twelve
THE REAL MIROIR

M s. Mayor. Hello!" Miroir tried to keep up his confident demeanor, but Ada could see he was shaken. "As I was saying to these girls, every artist has a style. . . ."

"Yes, and you steal it. The problem is, we were looking for an *original* painting for my office," said the mayor, "not a copy."

"Oh, my approach is *completely* original. You see, I like to *reflect* the art I see. . . ."

"Well, you can reflect it elsewhere," Ms. Lace said sternly. "I won't host an artist who steals, especially from one of our own."

Ada was impressed. Nina smiled smugly at Guy Miroir. Ada thought she could see her friend fighting to keep from sticking out her

tongue at him. And who could blame her?

"I'll ship your work to you, Guy." Ms. Lace glanced pointedly to the door.

"Fine!" Miroir yelled. "You all lack the talent and imagination to understand my work anyway!" He threw his scarf over his shoulder, ran out, and slammed the door behind him.

"Well. Now that *that's* out of the way," Ms. Lace said. She turned to the mayor. "I'm very sorry, Ms. Mayor. I'm sure we can find you a worthy replacement. One that's authentic."

"You know, Nina made the piece *Guy reflected in Gleam amidst the Gloom*. It's on her website," Ada said.

"It's called *Shine*," said Nina.

"Yes, I've seen it. When I was in here the other day, I admired that piece that your mother has over her desk." She pointed to a school project that Nina had given to Ms. Lace. "So I asked about the artist, and then I found your portfolio. I adore *Shine*. So much fresher than Miroir's copy. I'd love to see it up in my office every day," the mayor said to Nina.

"Oh my gosh! Thank you! This is the best day of my life!" Nina squealed, and then quickly composed herself. "I mean, ahem, yes, Ms. Mayor. I think we can have that arranged."

Chapter Thirteen
NEW BEGINNINGS

Ada had invited Nina to go hiking with her and Tycho, but Nina was too busy. She had been on fire since Miroir had left town. The *San Francisco Chronicle* received word about the stolen artwork. Journalists from the paper conducted their own investigation and published an exposé on Guy Miroir, detailing all the work he'd stolen over the years. Nina herself was interviewed in the piece, and Web traffic skyrocketed after that. Of course, having her artwork in the mayor's office didn't hurt either. The mayor was happy to tell the story behind the famous painting above her desk to anyone who would listen.

Ms. Lace had a lot of work to do after she'd essentially kicked Miroir and his paintings out of the gallery. After the news flurry around Miroir, she decided her next exhibit should highlight the work of artists he had stolen from. The exposé revealed this happened to nearly twenty artists from all over the world. Ms. Lace had her work cut out for her, but this time it was work she was happy to do.

Ada thought Tycho might suggest a nice easy trail in Golden Gate Park until he got used to the new wheels, but instead he suggested going to Mount Tamalpais. He was eager to try out the chair on a rugged trail. Ms. Lace volunteered to bring them. Ada hadn't seen her mom in such a good mood in weeks. She even raced Tycho and Ada over parts of the trail.

At first Ada was worried she might not be able to keep up. Tycho had been practicing around the courtyard enough so that he was one with his new creation. He flew over the straight parts of the trail. There were still some things that were tougher to navigate with wheels, so Ada was able to catch up.

"Looks like you've got the hang of that hand-cycle," said Ada. She took a minute to catch her breath. "This is turning into a workout for me."

"Oh, I'm a pro," said Tycho. "And I'm only getting faster. Soon you'll need one too. Or a mountain bike, because those feet of yours will be worn out in an hour running next to me."

Tycho was fun to hike with. They made a good team. Ada liked to stop and notice birds, flowers, different types of moss . . . but Tycho kept up the challenging pace. And he was the one who pointed out a gray whale when they passed a view of the ocean.

Ada gasped. "I didn't even know. . . ."

"Yeah, that's part of the reason I wanted to come here. I heard you might be able to see them migrating around now."

• • •

When they got back to Juniper Garden, Ada asked if Tycho wanted to come over for dinner, but he had to go home and pack. Ms. Lace headed inside while Ada stayed to talk to Tycho a little longer.

"When do you leave?" asked Ada.

"Pretty early in the morning. It's a long trip back to LA."

"Oh," said Ada. "Will you be back soon?"

"At least during summer vacation, but maybe before that. You know all those weird days we get off in May," said Tycho.

"Yeah," said Ada. She would miss Tycho. They'd gotten to be good friends over the last week. "What about when I run into another coding problem?"

"You can e-mail me! And we can FaceTime," said Tycho. "Don't worry. We'll stay friends, Ada Lace."

"I know we will, Tycho Wilson." She leaned down and hugged him. "Say hi to Uncle Mr. Peebles for me."

"I will," said Tycho. He rolled up the ramp and into the building.

• • •

Ada was dying to hear from Nina. The mayor had invited Nina and her mom over to her house. She wanted Nina to meet some of her politician friends who loved her painting. Plus, after everyone heard the story of the fraud Miroir, they all wanted to meet the girl who helped take him down. Nina was supposed to come to Ada's afterward for dinner.

"I just don't understand why we're letting Elliott cook," Ada said to her mom. "Haven't we all learned a lesson?"

"Dad says he's getting better, Ada," said Ms. Lace. "Let's just give him a chance."

Ada did not have high hopes. It smelled good, but smells could be deceiving.

Nina showed up at 6:30.

"I'm so hungry! The mayor had a lot of food, but I couldn't eat any of it. I had such a nervous tummy!"

Nina wanted to describe the mayor's house

in careful detail for Ada, but the main thing she remembered was that there was an Indian rug in the entryway and striped wallpaper somewhere. Honestly, Nina was so excited and talking so fast it was hard to keep up with her. She was just telling Ada about the plush pink bath mats when Elliott and Mr. Lace came out with a roast chicken.

"Roast chicken with corn bread stuffing and oysters!" announced Elliott.

The chicken was a beautiful golden brown color. Stuffing spilled out from inside, and roast vegetables were carefully arranged around the edge of the tray.

"Wait," said Ada. "Dad? You cooked?"

"Nope," said Mr. Lace. "It was pretty much all Elliott."

"Wow, Elliott," said Nina. She was seated in front of a Pterosaur. "This smells great!"

Ms. Lace carved the bird and served it. There was more chewing than talking after that. At the end of it all Nina and Ada cleared the table.

"So, Nina," said Mr. Lace. "I hear you have a new painting featured in Isabella's art gallery."

"Yes! I just finished it," said Nina. "My creative energies have really been flowing these past

"That's great," said Mr. Lace. "You'll probably be seeing even more Web traffic once the exhibit opens."

"Definitely," Ada chimed in. "I've been tracking it. We have people all over the world logging on to her site. About six thousand unique views a month right now. Many people from France and Germany."

Everyone looked at Ada, impressed.

"Well, it looks like you don't need Tycho's help anymore," Ms. Lace said.

"Yeah. I've gotten the hang of it. I'm hoping we can get traffic up to fifteen thousand views per month by the end of the year."

"I better learn to paint faster," said Nina.

"Maybe you can hire Miroir. I hear he's not doing anything," said Ada.

Ada nudged Nina, and her friend smiled.

Elliott walked in with a tray full of little dishes and set them on the table.

"Anyone up for some crème brûlée?"

Behind the Science

WEB DESIGN

Think of all the times you've been on the Internet and all of the different Web pages you've seen. Each of those pages had to be created and designed by someone (like Ada or Tycho!). To create a Web page from scratch, you need to learn a little bit of coding. Common website-coding languages have names like HTML, CSS, and JavaScript. These are the coding languages that Ada would be learning to help build Nina's website, Nina Nina Land. Ada would use these languages to tell the website what it should look like: what font it should use, how big the words should be, and what colors should show up on the screen. Because Nina is asking Ada to build a very interactive Web page, Ada will probably have to learn a little bit of other languages, like Ruby on Rails, Python, or PHP. Different computer languages are designed to do different things. Of course, Nina wants her website to be as unique and amazing as she is. So you can imagine how challenging (and maybe frustrating) it would be for Ada to need to learn so many new programming languages to build it for her! Are you interested in coding? If you're just starting out, playing with MIT's Scratch is a good start. You can find that at scratch.mit.edu.

Hand-Operated Elevator

Elevators have a very long history. In fact, very basic elevators were used as early as 336 B.C. in ancient Rome! Modern elevators that were designed with safety brakes came along much later, in the 1850s. Once elevators were safe, it completely changed the way buildings in big cities were designed. Why? Well, before elevators, you wouldn't want to make a building very tall, because people would have to climb too many steps to get to their apartments or offices. With elevators, engineers and architects could make buildings taller and taller! The elevator that is in Mr. Peebles's apartment is a special type of old elevator that uses pulleys and gears to allow the person riding inside to make the elevator go up and down. There aren't many of these left around, but you can find videos of hand-powered elevators in action on YouTube!

Handcycle

A handcycle is like a bicycle, but it has three wheels instead of two, and you power the bike with your hands instead of your feet. There are many different types of handcycles, but in Tycho's case, his had two wheels in the back and one wheel in the front. Because these bikes can be powered with your hands, handcycles can be ridden by people who are paralyzed from the waist down. In fact, handcycling is one of the newest competitions at the Paralympic Games. Some handcycles, like the one that Tycho and Mr. Peebles built, are designed to go off-road and tackle tough, mountainous terrain!

Coding Forums

Remember when Ada couldn't figure out how to code a specific feature that Nina wanted, and Tycho said he would check the coding forums for help? This was a clever idea, because programmers are great at helping each other, and oftentimes you can simply reuse someone else's work to solve your own problem. In other fields this might be considered cheating, but it's so common in programming, there are websites that exist for the purpose of sharing codes people have written. A good example is the code sharing website GitHub, where programmers post the code they've written and encourage others to use it. You don't always have to reinvent the wheel!

If you're a programmer with a question, like Ada and Tycho, there are other helpful websites you can go to where you can look for answers. Websites like Stack

Overflow and Reddit have a community of programmers who are constantly asking and answering questions about every programming language imaginable. Have you run into a problem you can't figure out? These websites may already have the answer you need!

WEB ANALYTICS

When you build your own website, you can use Web analytics to learn a bit about the people who are visiting your site. I made my own website called TheSpaceGal.com, and I like to use Web analytics to track how many people visit my website each week. You can see how many people come to your website and what they are clicking on. On my website, most people click on the *About* page! Ada, Nina, and Tycho used the Web analytics on Nina's website to find the IP addresses of the people visiting her site. Then they used those IP addresses to figure out where those visitors were coming from. Thank goodness Ada and Tycho knew a thing or two about Web analytics, or they may have never had the proof they needed to bust Mr. Miroir!

Acknowledgments

"If you're not outraged, you're not paying attention."

My high school history teacher, Dr. Seitz, told us that quote, which I didn't fully understand at the time. When you're younger, it's easy to believe that all is right with the world and the adults have everything taken care of. But that's not always the case, and it's okay to be mad about it. It's okay to speak up when you see something that you believe is wrong.

I want to thank everyone in my life who gave me the courage and confidence to speak up on topics that I care about and to stand up for people who needed an ally. Fighting for things you care about can be scary, and we all need a support system to keep on fighting. Tommy, Mom, Dad, Drew, and all my friends along the way—you're the support system that keeps on giving.

Thanks to the dream team who brought Ada's voice to life through these books—Tamson, Renee, Liz, Christian, Kyell, and Jennifer—Ada wouldn't be here without you.

And to all of you out there reading these books, thank you for welcoming Ada into your home. I hope that, like Ada, you'll always stay curious and keep exploring.